To Sue Tarsky and Carol Southern with thanks
KH   **and**   HC
Also love and thanks to Paul Craig for valuable advice
HC

Text © 1989 Katharine Holabird
Illustrations © 1989 Helen Craig

First published 1989 Aurum Books for Children
33 Museum Street, London WC1A 1LD

Printed in Hong Kong by Imago

British Library Cataloguing in Publication Data
Holabird, Katharine
I. Title II.   Craig, Helen
823′.914[J]
ISBN 1-85406-036-8

10 9 8 7 6 5 4 3 2 1

Angelina's Birthday

Illustrations by Helen Craig   Story by Katharine Holabird

Aurum Books for Children
London

Angelina loved her bicycle, and rode it everywhere. The bicycle had belonged to Aunt Amy and it was quite old, but Angelina thought that it was the best bicycle in the world.

One morning, she pedaled as fast as she could over to Alice's house.

"Next week will be my birthday and we're going to have a picnic!" Angelina announced to Alice. "My mother said we could go to the village today and buy decorations."

Alice jumped on her bicycle and they rode quickly down the road to Mrs. Thimble's General Store.

"Another birthday, Angelina!" Mrs. Thimble chuckled as she showed the girls the party decorations. "My, but you're getting old!" Angelina smiled proudly as she paid for the streamers and balloons. She really did feel a lot older now that she could ride her bike so well and was sent on important errands to the village.

"Come on, Angelina, let's have a race!" called Alice.

Angelina loved to race Alice down the bumpy road home. "I'll beat you, Alice!" Angelina shouted, going so fast that she didn't see the big rock lying directly in her path.

BANG!

The bike crashed into the rock.
Angelina flew into the air and
then fell to the ground with
a terrible bump.

"OOOOOOOOH! Why did you make me race, Alice!" cried Angelina angrily, pointing to a cut on her foot.

Poor Alice was very upset. She took Angelina's hand and helped her stand up. They looked at the bicycle. One wheel had come off, the other was twisted and the handlebars were upside down.

"Maybe we can fix it," said Alice.

They dragged the broken bicycle back to Angelina's house, where
Mr. Mouseling bandaged Angelina's foot and shook his head.
"That must have been quite a crash," he said.

"What shall I do?" Angelina asked sadly.

Mrs. Mouseling smiled at her. "Perhaps you're old enough
now to help earn some money to buy a new bicycle."

"I'll try," Angelina agreed, and she made
a list of all the jobs she could do.
Alice offered to help.

On Monday after school, Angelina
planted strawberries and
raspberries for Mrs. Hodgepodge.

On Tuesday afternoon, Angelina
helped her ballet teacher, Miss
Lilly, wash the dance floor and
polish the piano.

On Wednesday, Angelina and Alice watered the garden and
hung out the washing for Alice's mother, who had a new baby.

On Thursday, they mowed the grass and picked apples for Angelina's grandparents.

On Friday, Angelina and Alice helped Mr. Bell, the old postman, repair and paint his front door. Then they walked to Mrs. Thimble's store for more balloons.

Angelina was happy. She felt so proud of their hard work and the money they had earned. Then they passed the bicycle shop. There in the window was the most beautiful bicycle Angelina had ever seen. But it was very expensive. Angelina counted all her money. "I haven't even got enough to buy a nice horn for that bike."

"I wish I could buy the bicycle for you," said Alice.

Saturday afternoon was Angelina's birthday party.
Alice came early to help blow up the balloons
and decorate the garden. Angelina's mother and
Aunt Amy had made a delicious picnic, and soon
Angelina's friends started arriving.

Flora and Felicity brought Angelina hair ribbons
and a book on dancing. Alice gave her a delicate
ballerina doll. Cousin Henry gave Angelina a
silver horn for when she got another bicycle.
Angelina managed to smile and hug Henry
because she knew that he was trying to be kind.

The party games began. The garden filled with singing voices,
"HAPPY BIRTHDAY, ANGELINA!
HAPPY BIRTHDAY TO YOU . . ."
Angelina saw her grandparents, followed by Mrs. Hodgepodge, Miss Lilly,
Mrs. Thimble, Alice's mother, Mr. Bell and Aunt Amy, all with bicycles!
"We came to have a race with you, Angelina," said her grandmother.

Angelina was surprised. "I'd love to go," she said,
"but I don't have a new bike yet," and she felt like crying.

"Angelina! Come and look!" shouted Henry,
who had a terrible time keeping secrets.

And there, hidden behind the garden shed, was the shiny new bicycle that Angelina and Alice had seen in the village.

"Oh!" Angelina was so excited that she jumped on the bicycle and rode it in circles around and around the garden. Her grandfather smiled at her and said, "You and Alice worked so hard that we all wanted to help buy the bicycle for your birthday."

Then Angelina led everyone on a birthday bicycle ride over the hills, singing all the way, with balloons and streamers flying in the wind.